Shadow the Secret Pony

A sharp, snapping noise made Clare open her eyes. It sounded like a stick breaking. The noise came from the bottom of the garden.

"Oh!" Clare gasped. There, standing in front of a mass of trees and bushes, was a black pony!

Titles in Jenny Dale's PONY TALES™ series

All of Jenny Dale's PONY TALES books can be ordered at your local bookshop or are available by post from Book Service by Post (tel: 01624 675137)

Shadow the Secret Pony

by Jenny Dale

Illustrated by Frank Rodgers

A Working Partners Book

MACMILLAN CHILDREN'S BOOKS

Special thanks to Linda Chapman

First published 2000 by Macmillan Children's Books
a division of Macmillan Publishers Limited
25 Eccleston Place, London SW1W 9NF
Basingstoke and Oxford
www.macmillan.co.uk

Associated companies throughout the world

Created by Working Partners Limited
London W6 0QT

ISBN 0 330 37474 5

Copyright © Working Partners Limited 2000
Illustrations copyright © Frank Rodgers 2000

JENNY DALE'S PONY TALES is a trade mark
owned by Working Partners Ltd.

135798642

A CIP catalogue record for this book is available from
the British Library.

Typeset by SX Composing DTP, Rayleigh, Essex
Printed and bound in Great Britain by Mackays of Chatham plc, Kent

Chapter One

Clare Masters sat in the garden of her new home, looking at a picture in a pony magazine. It showed three ponies grazing in a field. Clare tried to decide which pony she liked best. The grey one had a pretty face. The golden palomino had a lovely long mane and tail. But the black one looked really sweet and friendly . . .

Clare let the magazine flop onto the grass and shut her eyes. She began to daydream that the black pony was hers. Every day after school they would ride out into the woods. They jumped and galloped and . . .

Crack!

A sharp, snapping noise made Clare open her eyes. It sounded like a stick breaking.

Crack! Crack!

The noise came from the bottom of the garden. "Oh!" Clare gasped. There, standing in front of a mass of trees and bushes, was a black pony!

The pony looked at her, then

stepped forward, snorting.
Another couple of twigs snapped
underneath his hooves. *Crack!*
Crack!

Clare rubbed her eyes. There
couldn't really be a black pony in
the garden, could there? But when
she looked again, the pony was
still there – coal-black all over,
apart from four white socks.

The pony whinnied and trotted over to Clare.

Clare's heart thumped hard as the pony circled round her. She felt his warm breath on her cheeks, and was finally sure that he was a real, live pony.

She scrambled to her feet and held out her hand. "Where have you come from?" she whispered.

The pony nudged her hand, looking hopefully for treats. When he found nothing he turned his head away, disappointed.

Clare guessed what the pony wanted. She hurried to a nearby apple tree, pulled an apple off the lowest branch and offered it to him.

The pony took it gently from the palm of her hand, crunching it happily and blowing bits of apple at Clare.

Clare laughed and patted the pony on his warm, soft neck. She couldn't believe she was standing there with a real pony in her garden. Excitement bubbled up through her. "Wait here," she told him. "I'm going to get Mum."

Giving the pony one last stroke, Clare ran up the garden and into the house. "Mum!" she shouted. "Mum! Come quick!"

Mrs Masters was upstairs. She appeared at the top of the staircase. "What's the matter, Clare?" she asked quickly. "Have you hurt yourself?"

"No!" Clare was so excited that she could hardly get the words out. "I'm fine. But there's a *pony* in the garden!"

The worried look left Mrs Masters' face. "You and your imaginary ponies, Clare," she said, smiling.

"This one's *not* imaginary!" Clare raced up the stairs. "Quick, Mum! Come and see!"

"I'm in the middle of unpacking!" Mrs Masters said. "I can't play right now, Clare."

"But I'm not playing. He's real!" Clare cried in frustration. "You can see from that window!" She tugged her mum across the landing towards the window that looked out on to the back garden. "Look!"

Mrs Masters looked out.

"He's by the . . ." Clare's voice suddenly trailed off. *The pony wasn't there!* "Oh, he's gone!" she cried in dismay.

"Oh, Clare," Mrs Masters said, shaking her head. "I should know better. For a moment there, you almost had me thinking I was about to see a real pony."

"But there *was* one," Clare cried.

"He was standing by the trees. I fed him an apple."

Her mum smiled. "Well, why don't you go and feed him another one. Now, I'm going to get on with that unpacking."

"But Mum . . ." Clare protested. She could see that her mum thought the pony was just imaginary.

Clare gave up and ran down the stairs. The pony *couldn't* have just disappeared.

She hurried outside to check the side gate. But it was shut and locked. The pony couldn't have got out there. She looked behind the shed. He wasn't there, either. As Clare was wondering where to look next, an upstairs window opened.

"Clare!" her mum called out. "Come and get your school things ready for tomorrow, please. I don't want you to be late in the morning. Not on your first day at a new school."

"But, Mum, I'm looking for the pony!" Clare called back.

"You can look for him later," Mrs Masters said firmly.

"But, Mum . . . !" Clare protested.

"*Now*, Clare!"

Clare knew that tone of voice. It meant, *do as you are told or else . . .*

Shooting one last look round the garden Clare hurried inside and up to her bedroom – which was very untidy. She and her mum had only moved into their new house three days ago and they still hadn't unpacked everything. Toys and books spilled out of cardboard boxes piled high on the floor.

Clare sat down beside one of the boxes and quickly started searching through it. The sooner she found her school things, the sooner she could get outside and carry on looking for the pony.

She found her pencil case and threw it on to her bed. It was strange to think about starting at a new school. It was going to be really weird not knowing anyone. She pulled a packet of felt tips out of the box. She hoped she was going to make friends.

Jumping to her feet, Clare went

to the wardrobe and pulled out
her new school sweatshirt and
black trousers. She glanced out of
the window at the back garden.
The pony *had* been real. So where
had he gone?

Chapter Two

The next morning, Clare walked with her mum to her new school.

Mrs Masters gave Clare a quick kiss and a hug. "Have a good day," she said, handing Clare her lunch box. "Your drink's in your bag. And there's a packet of crisps for break time. I'll be waiting at the gates for you after school."

Clare had visited her new classroom and met Mrs Bennett, her new teacher, a few weeks ago. But now, as she watched her new classmates talking and laughing loudly, she felt shy. Her fingers tightened around the handle of her lunch box.

"Hello, Clare," said a friendly voice.

Clare looked round. Mrs Bennett had come into the classroom. Clare smiled, feeling a little better.

"Let's get started, shall we?" Mrs Bennett said briskly. She asked everyone to sit down, and introduced Clare. Then she picked out a girl with a long, blonde ponytail. "Lisa, I would like you to look after Clare until she gets to know where things are. She'll be sitting at your table."

"Yes, Miss," the girl with the ponytail said.

Clare went over to take the spare place at Lisa's table.

After doing the register, it was time for maths. Mrs Bennett gave Clare a new book to work in.

Clare started to write her name on the cover of the book, like she'd been shown at her old school.

"Not there!" Lisa told her bossily. "Write it at the bottom."

Clare took out her rubber.

"And we're not allowed to rub out," Lisa said quickly. "We have to cross things out if we make a mistake."

Clare crossed her name out and wrote it at the bottom.

Lisa looked at her crossing out and frowned. "You should have used a ruler."

Clare bit her lip. She seemed to be doing *everything* wrong.

"Here." One of the other girls at the table offered Clare a ruler. "If you go over it, you'll hardly be able to tell." She smiled shyly. "I'm Matty, by the way."

Clare smiled back and took the ruler. It had little pictures of horses on it. "Do you like horses?" she asked Matty eagerly.

Matty suddenly looked uncomfortable. She glanced across at Lisa and the other girl.

"Horses are banned on this table!" Lisa said. "They are so boring!"

After school, Clare found her mum waiting for her at the school gates.

"Well? How was it?" Mrs Masters asked eagerly.

"Horrible," Clare said. She was

feeling miserable. All day she had seemed to get things wrong, and Lisa had been very bossy. Matty and Faye, the other two girls on the table, hadn't spoken much to her either.

Mrs Masters looked at Clare's downcast face. "It will get better, love," she said, putting an arm round Clare's shoulders. "It's always difficult settling in to a new school. You'll soon make friends."

Clare didn't feel so sure. Everyone else in the class seemed to have made their friends already. No one seemed to want a new friend.

As soon as she arrived home, Clare changed out of her school clothes and ran out into the garden. She found an apple tree with low branches and climbed up. She felt very upset. It wasn't fair, she thought. Why did they have to move house? Why couldn't she have stayed at her old school?

It was peaceful in the tree. Clare closed her eyes. She could hear the sounds of birds chirping and the leaves rustling in the breeze. She wished that she could stay there for ever.

Crack! Crack!

Clare's eyes flew open. That noise! She looked down and almost fell out of the tree in surprise. Standing underneath her was the black pony!

Chapter Three

"Hello," the pony neighed happily.

Clare gasped, then scrambled down from the tree and patted the pony. His neck was warm and solid. "Hello, boy! You came back!" Clare pulled an apple off the tree and offered it to the pony.

He nuzzled against her. "Mmm, lovely! The apples aren't too sour in this garden," he snorted.

Clare wondered how the pony had got into the garden. She went over to check the side gate again. But it was locked.

The pony followed her, his nose nudging against her back.

Clare laughed. "You're like a shadow," she said. She stopped and looked at his gleaming dark coat. "That's what I'd call you if you were mine," she whispered. "Shadow."

The pony started to nibble Clare's hair. She laughed and pushed him away.

Shadow trotted back down to the apple trees. He started to

nibble an old apple that was lying on the ground.

"Don't eat that, it's rotten," Clare said, seeing the black skin on the apple. She hurried over to stop him.

Shadow tossed his head playfully and trotted away. He stopped behind a tree and peeped out at her. "Come and get me!" he whinnied.

Clare laughed and ran up to him. Shadow let her get close enough almost to touch him and then jumped away and trotted over to another tree. "You can't catch me!" he snorted happily.

Clare ran faster and so did Shadow. He broke into a canter, swerving behind a tree, stopping dead and looking back at her before setting off again. "This is fun!" he whinnied.

After a while, Clare's cheeks were pink and she was out of breath. "I can't run any more!" she called. She sat down on the grass.

Shadow came out from behind the tree trunk where he was hiding and walked over to Clare. Stretching his neck towards her, he blew on her hair. "I like playing with you," he whickered.

Clare giggled at the feel of Shadow's warm breath. She stroked his muzzle and wondered where he had come from and who owned him. He must belong to someone. His coat was very shiny and he looked well fed.

"I'd better get Mum," she said, standing up and hugging the pony. "Your owner might be looking for you."

But Clare didn't want to leave him. She wondered if Shadow's owner might let her come and visit him some time. Life wouldn't be nearly so bad then. Well, except for school, she thought, her heart sinking.

Clare buried her face in Shadow's warm, furry neck. "Oh, Shadow, I hate my new school," she said. "I haven't got any friends there. I wish I didn't have to go back!"

Shadow pricked his ears. His owner was always saying how much she hated school too.

"School doesn't sound much fun!" he snorted. He nuzzled Clare, hoping it would make her feel better. It always worked with his owner.

Clare laughed and hugged Shadow tighter. "I wish you were my pony," she said. "If you were my pony then even school wouldn't seem so bad."

She sighed. She knew she really should tell her mum that the pony was in the garden. "Wait here," she said, patting his neck. "I'm going to get Mum and she'll help find your owner."

Shadow watched Clare run into the house. Suddenly he heard a faint sound in the distance. He knew that voice. Pricking up his ears, he turned and trotted down the garden.

Clare dragged her mum out of the kitchen. "Clare, I'm busy!" Mrs Masters cried.

"But there's a pony in the garden!" Clare said. "There really is! We'll have to try and find out who he belongs to." She pushed open the back door. "Look!" She stopped.

Shadow had gone.

"But he was here!" Clare cried. "He *was*! He followed me round the garden and we played hide and seek . . ."

Mrs Masters put an arm around Clare's shoulders. "Oh, Clare. I know it's hard, moving house and changing schools. I can see why you might want to make up a pony friend, but—"

"I'm not making him up!" Clare cried. "He's real!" But she could see that her mum didn't believe her. Tears of frustration came into her eyes. "He is, Mum!"

"Why don't you come inside?" Mrs Masters said gently. "I'll

make you a chocolate milkshake."

But Clare shook her head and ran back out into the garden. She knew Shadow was real. So where had he gone? He couldn't have just vanished. The gate was shut, so the pony must be getting in and out of the garden some other way. If she could just find out how, then maybe her mum would believe her.

Clare checked all the fences, but there seemed to be no gaps big enough for a pony to squeeze through. She ran down to the bottom of the garden, where she'd first seen Shadow. Behind the apple trees and bushes Clare could see a row of tall, dark green conifer trees. Where exactly did the garden end? She decided to explore.

Clare pushed her way through the thick, overgrown bushes, over to the row of conifers. She squeezed between two of the trees to see what was behind them. The feathery fronds of their branches tickled her face.

Behind the trees was a fence. Clare had come to the end of the garden. Suddenly she noticed that one part of the fence had a gap in it – a gap big enough for a pony to get through . . .

Clare's heart leaped. She scrambled through the gap and came out into a large field. Perhaps this was where Shadow lived!

Chapter Four

As she looked around, Clare saw
that the field was empty. Shadow
wasn't there after all.

Sadly, Clare turned round and
pushed her way back into the
garden. Her shoulders sagged
with disappointment. She had
really wanted Shadow to live in

the field beyond her garden.

She sighed and crossed her fingers that he would visit her again soon.

Clare's heart still felt heavy as she walked to school the next morning. In the classroom she saw that Matty was sitting at her table. Lisa and Faye had not arrived yet.

Clare went over and sat down.

Matty smiled. "Hi," she said.

"Hi," Clare said back, feeling better. Matty was much friendlier than Lisa or Faye. She watched Matty drawing a straight line with her ruler. It was the same one as the day before – the one with pictures of horses on it.

Clare frowned. "Why have you

got that ruler?" she asked.

Matty looked up. "What do you mean?"

"If you don't like horses, why have you got a ruler with those pictures on?" Clare said.

"But I do like horses," Matty said. Her cheeks went pink. She dropped her head as if she was embarrassed. "I . . . I've got my own pony."

Clare stared in astonishment. "You've got a pony!"

Matty nodded. "Yes."

Clare could hardly believe that Matty had a pony of her own. Why hadn't she said anything about it the day before? Clare knew that if she had a pony she would talk about it all the time!

"What's he like?" Clare cried.
"How big is he?" The questions
burst forth. "What colour?"

Matty looked at Clare
uncertainly. "Do you like ponies?"

"I love them!" Clare said.

Matty's face lit up. "He's . . ."

Just then Lisa and Faye came in
and sat down at the table.

"I hope you're not talking about
that pony of yours, Matty," Lisa
said. "Boring!"

Matty flushed red and looked
down, her mouth tightly shut.

Clare turned to Matty. "*I* don't
think having a pony is boring,"
she said. "How long have you had
him? Can he jump?"

"No pony talk!" Lisa said
bossily. "It's the rule!"

Clare looked at Matty, but she didn't seem to want to talk.

For the rest of the day Lisa and Faye were always there, and no one talked about ponies.

But after school, as Clare walked home with her mum, Matty came hurrying up beside her. She looked a bit nervous. "Would you

. . . would you like to come to tea tomorrow?" she asked. "You could come and see my pony."

Clare was astonished. "Come and see your pony!"

"Only if you'd like to, of course," Matty said, going pink.

"Like to? I'd *love* to!" Clare exclaimed. She turned to her mum. "I can, can't I, Mum?"

Mrs Masters nodded, smiling. "It sounds fun," she said.

For the first time since Clare had met her, Matty grinned, her brown eyes shining. "Great! See you tomorrow then!" she said, hurrying away.

"See you!" Clare called back.

Mrs Masters looked at Clare. "You're looking a bit happier," she said. "What's Matty like?"

Clare thought. "She's quite quiet and a bit shy," she said. Then she remembered the cheerful grin that Matty had given her. "But I think she might be OK."

As soon as she got home, Clare ran upstairs to change out of her uniform. Her heart was beating fast. Would Shadow turn up again today?

She hurried out through the back door and down to the bottom of the garden. "Shadow!" she called softly.

Nothing happened.

"Shadow!" Clare called again. She shut her eyes. *Please come!* she whispered. *Please!*

But when Clare opened her eyes there was still no sign of the pony. Her heart sank. She turned away and sighed sadly. Maybe Shadow wouldn't ever come again.

Crack! Crack!

Clare turned back to look. And there was Shadow, coming through the trees.

Chapter Five

"Shadow!" Clare cried. She ran up and flung her arms around the pony's neck. "You've come!"

"Of course!" Shadow whinnied. He nudged her. "Should we play hide and seek again?" With a toss of his head, he trotted off and hid behind a tree.

Clare laughed happily and soon they were playing as if Shadow hadn't been away.

At last, Clare was out of breath and stopped. "Oh, Shadow!" she said. "Having you here is almost as good as having my own pony!"

Then an idea struck her. If Shadow was going to come and visit every day then she could pretend he *was* her own pony. She could get a brush for him and groom him and she could make a head collar for him. Of course, she wouldn't be able to ride him, but looking after him would be almost as good.

"You'll be my secret pony!" she said.

Shadow nuzzled her. "That

sounds fun," he snorted.

Clare remembered her news. "There's a girl at school with a pony," she said. "She's invited me round to tea tomorrow. She's called Matty."

Shadow's ears pricked up. But just as he was about to whicker something, Mrs Masters called

Clare in for her tea.

"Bye, Shadow," Clare whispered. She kissed him and ran happily up the garden. It really was just like having a pony of her own!

The next day at school, Matty kept looking across the table at Clare and grinning at her. Neither of them had said anything to Lisa and Faye about the invitation to tea. Clare was glad they didn't know. She had a feeling that they wouldn't be pleased.

After school Matty came running up to Clare. "Hi!" she said breathlessly. "Are you ready?"

Clare nodded. She had her school bag and a bag with jeans

and an old sweatshirt in it.

They hurried outside. Matty's mum was waiting by the gates. She smiled at Clare. "Hello," she said. "I'm Mrs Davies. So you're coming for tea with us – and to meet Socks."

Clare smiled back at Mrs Davies, then turned to Matty. "Socks – is that your pony's name?" she asked.

Matty nodded. As they walked along, she pointed to a gravel track that led up the hill. "I keep him in a field up there," she said. "But when it gets colder we'll have to find stables for him to live in."

"Will he like that?" Clare asked.

"I think so," Matty said. "He'll like having other ponies around."

"He's on his own at the moment, you see," Mrs Davies explained. "And we think he must get a bit bored."

Clare looked at the track that led to Socks's field. "Can we go and see him right now?" she asked eagerly.

Mrs Davies shook her head, smiling. "You've got to go to school tomorrow in those clothes," she said. "You'd better get changed first. There'll be plenty of time after tea."

As soon as they got to the Davieses' house, Matty ran up the stairs. "Come on, let's get changed."

Clare followed her. "Wow!" she

said, looking round Matty's bedroom. The walls were covered with pony posters.

"I've always loved ponies," Matty said.

Clare frowned. "So why don't you ever talk about them at school?"

Matty bit her lip. "Because of Lisa and Faye." She sighed. "I only came to the school last term. Lisa and Faye made friends with me but they said they didn't want to talk about horses. I thought it was better being friends with them than being on my own."

Clare sat down on Matty's bed. "They're a bit bossy."

"*Very* bossy," Matty agreed. She looked shyly at Clare. "But *we*

49

could be friends."

Clare grinned. "We could!"

They started to get changed.

"You're so lucky having your own pony," Clare said.

"I'd wanted one for ages," Matty said, pulling on some jodhpurs. She looked at Clare. "Promise you won't laugh?"

Clare nodded.

"Well, I used to want one so much that I used to *pretend* I had a pony – a secret pony." Matty's cheeks went a bit red. "Do you think that's silly?"

Clare's eyes opened wide in surprise. "No!" she cried. She looked at Matty and decided to share her own secret. "As a matter of fact, *I've* got a secret pony!" she said. "But it's not a made-up one. He's a real pony who comes into my garden."

"A *real* secret pony?" said Matty.

"Yes!" Clare said. "He's come to play with me three times now."

"What's he like?" Matty asked, amazed.

"He's all black, except for his

four white socks," Clare told her. "He's gorgeous. He plays hide and seek with me and . . ." Clare saw Matty start to frown. "What's the matter?"

Matty stood up quickly. "That's Socks!" she cried angrily.

Clare was confused. "What do you mean?" she said.

"There's only one black pony with four white socks around here," Matty said. "And that's my Socks! What have you been doing with him?"

"Nothing!" Clare cried, jumping to her feet. "I'm not talking about your Socks! I'm talking about my Shadow!"

The bedroom door opened. Mrs Davies looked in. "Whatever's

going on here?"

Matty turned to her mum. "Clare says that she's got a secret pony just like Socks – but she can't have!"

"I'm not making it up!" Clare cried. "And my pony isn't Socks. He's Shadow!"

"He's not. He's Socks!"

Mrs Davies held up her hands. "Girls!" Matty and Clare looked at her. She seemed very confused. "I don't think I quite understand. But maybe it would help to go and see Socks straight away. Tea's not ready yet anyway."

Clare and Matty nodded. They pulled on the rest of their clothes and went downstairs.

"Don't be long," Mrs Davies

said. She smiled. "Socks will be surprised to see you this early, Matty."

Matty didn't smile. She marched off down the lane.

Clare hurried along beside her. She wished she'd never told Matty about Shadow. She should have just kept quiet.

Matty turned up a track and marched up to a gate that led into a field. "Now, try and tell me that you haven't been making up stories about Socks," she said. She pointed into the field. "Look!"

Clare stared around the field. It was empty. She looked at Matty.

Then Matty saw that the

field was empty too. "Socks!" she gasped. "Oh, no! He's gone!"

Chapter Six

Matty opened the gate and ran into the field. "Socks!" she called. "Socks!"

But no pony came. "He's escaped!" Matty said, turning to Clare, her face scared. "What if he's been run over! Suppose he's been stolen!"

Clare forgot about their argument. "Quick! Let's check the fences. There might be a gap where he could have got out!"

They ran round the field, looking for holes in the fence. As they reached the far end, Clare noticed a row of conifers growing nearby. They looked very like the ones growing at the bottom of her garden.

She stopped, and looked at the field again. That's it! she thought. She'd seen this field before, but from a very different angle . . .

"What are you waiting for?" Matty cried.

"It's OK!" Clare called. "I think I know where he is."

"What do you mean?" Matty said.

Clare didn't answer. She ran towards the conifers and looked along the fence in front of them. Sure enough, there was a big gap – just the right size for a pony. "This way!" she shouted.

Matty saw what she was looking at. Together they went through the gap.

"But where are we going?" asked Matty.

"My house," Clare said.

"Your house!" Matty echoed.

"My house is this side of the fence!" Clare pushed her way through the familiar yellow-green fronds of the conifers. "And I think I know just where Socks will be."

Matty followed her. "But . . . but . . ."

As they came out through the trees, Clare stopped. Just as she had thought, there was the pony, standing underneath one of the apple trees, munching on fallen apples.

"Socks!" Matty gasped.

"Or Shadow," Clare said.

"Whichever you like!" whinnied the black pony. He trotted over and nuzzled them. "Hello!"

Clare started to laugh.

It only took a moment before Matty joined in. "I wondered why he had been getting so fat," she said, through her laughter. "He must have been coming here

every day to eat your apples."

"And I couldn't work out where he kept disappearing to!" said Clare. "He must have come here while you were having your tea and squeezed back through the fence when it was time for you to come and ride him."

"Oh, Socks!" Matty said, hugging him. "You are a naughty pony."

Clare looked at Shadow nuzzling Matty and suddenly felt sad. She guessed this would mean that Shadow wouldn't be her secret pony any more.

Matty saw Clare's face. "Now we're friends you can come and help me look after him. Maybe you can ride him sometimes too," she said.

Clare stared at her in astonishment. "You mean it?"

"Of course!" Matty said. "It will be loads more fun if there are two of us."

"So we're still friends?" Clare said rather uncertainly.

Matty grinned. "Of course. After all, we were both right in a way. You were talking about Socks all the time – you just didn't realise it! So . . . friends?"

Clare grinned back. "Best friends!"

Just then, the back door opened. "Clare!" Mrs Masters came hurrying out, looking as if she couldn't believe her eyes. "What's going on?" she asked, looking at Matty and Clare and the pony.

Clare and Matty started to explain. They both talked at once, but soon Mrs Masters began to understand. "So there was a real pony after all!" she said.

Clare nodded. "He just kept disappearing to get back to see Matty."

Matty laughed. "But now Clare is going to come and help me look after him. He'll like that, won't you, Socks?"

Socks nuzzled at Clare's hair. "Sure will!"

Clare stroked him. She couldn't believe that she was going to be able to help look after him every day. It was like a dream come true.

"You'll have to get used to

calling him Socks though," Matty said, smiling.

Clare nodded. Yes, she would have to get used to the new name. She kissed Socks on the nose. But he would always be Shadow to her.